Devil's Sweetheart

Lexi Gray

Thank you!

Dedication

My lovelies...this isn't like my usual writing, I know. We're mixing it up a smidge with a softer, sweeter story to cleanse the palate(ish)!

Don't worry though, it's going to be *almost* as dirty.

For you.

Blurb

Birdie

Being friends is easy. There's no strings, no weird after math. Just simply coexisting together in a town that will siphon your money for rent alone. Being friends means we can talk about our latest hookups, even if they ended badly. We can talk about our families, our lives, how our day is...everything without complication. Then I opened my eyes. If I had to exist without him, it wouldn't be one worth living. He completes me. Only, I may have waited too long to tell him.

Scout

She's never noticed me. I make a move then get pushed right back into the pit of friendship. I can't tell if it's on purpose, or simply because we've known each other almost all of our lives. We were in diapers together, learned to walk and talk. Even had the same teachers throughout school. She's my world. I wouldn't exist without her. She wonders why I'm so put off by others...I only see her.

Chapter One

BIRDIE

The backroads leading to the vineyard are silent, minus the breeze that echoes through the leaves of the trees. Said roads are covered completely in snow and ice, the sides of the dirt road almost piled as tall as me.

It's later than I'd like it to be, but we all know the saying 'duty calls'. A known client decided to stop by late in the afternoon, and the VP of Sales, Viviana, asked that I stay back and assist. Something about my innocent face and ability to charm older men.

Right after she asked me, I took a bathroom break to text Scout. He's usually the one that gets me to and from work. After about ten minutes, there still wasn't a response. Looking at his location, I completely forgot that he was covering a late night shift tonight at Rusty's Dive Bar. The little joint is slowly transforming from a mom and pop dive bar to another classic chic location.

Now, just after midnight, I still don't have a response. It's a Friday night which so happens to be the weekend before Valentine's day. Hopefully he's making good tips off the single college girls around town. That man has abs for days, and I've debated on wrecking our friendship just to be able to lick them myself.

Bad news is that I'm going to have to walk several miles to get into town in the pitch darkness and woods. That would only be the walk to Rusty's. Living in the bum fuck boonies of Gideon Lake, where the projects meet the slums, I worry about everything. Buses don't even run this late, and there aren't any available Ubers near me. If I paid for an Uber out here, it'd be an arm and a leg. So, I either walk to the bar and be an inconvenience or I call Scout and be an inconvenience. In an awkward debate between me, myself, and I, we all agree to not bother Scout. Exercise is always good for the heart and body. Just thinking about calling him for a ride gives me freaking heart palpitations. Honestly, it's worse than a bad orgasm.

The longer I walk, the more time my brain has to conjure up scenarios of torment. It wasn't too long ago that something of mine was taken away from me without permission in a situation much like this one...

"Stop it," I croak to myself. "You don't need others, put your damn big girl panties on." Even as I try to give myself a pep-talk, all I can think about is the things *he* did to me.

The shroud of darkness feels near suffocating. And when a car horn *beeps* at me, I damn near jump out of my skin.

"Birdie?" Sofia shouts, leaning over Massimo in the driver's seat. A tight lipped smile extends on my cheeks, an awkward wave in salute.

"Yup, that's me," I chuckle oddly. Unsure what to do with myself, I shove my hands back into my pockets and kick a rock.

"Oh gosh, girl! You aren't freezing?" She exclaims loudly, shoving at Massimo to put the car in park. My mouth drops open, then slams closed. An action I repeat over and over again because I have no clue what's going on.

"Uhm, no," I draw out, more like a question. Rounding the car, she gathers me in her arms and ushers me to the car. I can't do anything besides follow her lead. The stammering in my chest is back, the feeling of being an inconvenience suddenly overwhelming. "You don't have to give me a ride, I'm not that far away."

"Nonsense," Massimo booms, cutting me off. "I've seen your apartment. Not only do you live nearly twenty miles out, but it's almost freezing outside. Get in the car." My muscles snap into action as I push forward to get into the vehicle. Like a damn control switch flicked, I can't *not* do what he's telling me.

Shutting the door softly behind me, Sofia rounds back to the passenger seat. "Why didn't you tell us you didn't have a ride?" She asks, obviously annoyed but concerned.

"Oh, well, I didn't-it wasn't-Scout was-," I stumble over myself trying to come up with a valid reason as to why I was walking.

"Birdie." Our eyes snap to Massimo, who meets mine through the mirror. "You act as if we aren't familiar with you. The terror you felt? I saw it bleeding from your eyes. We *know* you. Remember that." Putting the car in drive, the rest of our journey is utterly silent.

He's not wrong though. It was the talk of the town for a while that I pursued charges against *him*. If it weren't for Scout...

Shaking my head, I don't really want to think about that. Street lights suddenly come into view, then they're whizzing by. There's no real point in trying to focus on the things around me when Scout plagues most of my thoughts. Whether they're good thoughts like how badly I want to kiss him, or ones about how he saved me from myself, they just seem to drift back to him.

Three years ago, I'd imagined saving myself for marriage. My husband was going to be the person to have me in my entirety. Not because of religion, just that I wanted to be able to give my life partner the best gift of all. Then, it was taken from me. Ripped out of my hands by a stranger with a vendetta against the man I've had a crush on for almost my whole life.

Weirdly, I've planned Scout and I's wedding since the beginning. Then, after everything happened, I decided that being solo is better than having someone take something you've dreamed of away from you. I never want to experience that dread again.

"Birdie, we're here," Sofia calls, bursting me out of my bubble.

"Oh," I mumble, the street lights no longer moving as we pull up outside Scout and I's complex. "Thank you. I appreciate it." She reaches backward and gives my hand an almost motherly squeeze. There's not a huge age difference, maybe only six or seven years, but it's reassuring nonetheless.

"You know we're here for you." Pulling her hand away, Massimo gets out of the car and opens the door for me. A slight blush creeps over my cheeks at the chivalry. It's a dying breed, but not for men who were raised in blood shed.

"Call if you need anything." They wait until I get to my front door and unlock it before driving away. Darkness shrouds over me once more as I step into the entryway. Leaving the lights off, I toe off my shoes and head straight for the room. My body drags with me as exhaustion sets in.

Showering be damned, I'm going to bed.

Chapter Two

SCOUT

Rusty's is booming with folks of all ages. The cranky regulars bitch about the music playing on the jukebox while the college crowd spins around rhythmically. Grabbing the wash rag, I wipe away the small liquid droplets and place the finger full of whiskey in front of Paul.

"Man, you know these kids just keep getting sluttier and sluttier," he grunts, bringing the drink to his lips and slamming it back. I can't help but laugh. My phone rings in my pocket. Drying my hands, I pull it out and catch an unknown number. I mute the device and place it on the counter.

"You not going to get that?" Dennis grunts, sloshing his own tumbler as the device buzzes loudly. The same unknown number flashes across my screen before disappearing. Seconds later, it pops back up. Sighing heavily, I grab it and make my way outside.

"Cupid, I'm going on break!" I shout down the bar, not waiting for a reply. We're not super busy since we're getting closer and closer to closing time, but I figure it's better than leaving him without any warning at all.

Stepping into the cool air of Coal's Lake, my phone buzzes harshly in my palm. "Yo?" I call, leaning myself against the brick wall of the bar.

"Scout Ashbluff?" A gruff voice askes.

"Who's asking?" The voice sounds awfully familiar, and I can't quite place who but my spine straightens painfully as I try to remember.

"This is Massimo, owner of Vinonova Vineyard," he starts, and a female voice snaps at them from the background. A small ruffling happens before said female takes the phone.

"Hi, this is Sofia. I got your number from Birdie's emergency contact list, it has you as her roommate. My husband and I wanted to tell you that we dropped her off at your place in Gideon Lake." My brow furrows as I try to recall talking with Birdie. Pulling the phone away from my ear, I realize it's just past one in the morning. There are several texts from Birdie through the evening.

The ride to Gideon Lake is several miles from here, let alone another fifteen miles outside of town. We'd been slammed at the bar tonight, and I hadn't gotten a chance to even tell her to call me when she needed a ride. Cursing softly, I put the phone back to my ear.

"Thank you for ensuring she made it home safely," I thank them, my tone filled with absolute gratitude. I've failed as a friend.

"Gosh," she scoffs, and I swear I can hear a head shake. "Can you believe she was trying to *walk*? We damn near had to kidnap her just to give her a ride!"

"I'm actually not surprised," I mutter, running my hand through my hair. The air is chilly, and my breaths come out in puffs of air.

"Either way, just wanted to let you know." We say our quick goodbyes before I finally read through all of her messages.

> Hey! Just letting you know I'm going to be late tonight. Some big wig is showing up

> Ooooh, it was some dude from TokTok wanting to get samples. Freeloaders.

> Are you busy at work?

> I'm taking your silence as a yes lol I'll let you know when I get home.

> I'm off work, are you free?

> Again, silence as a sign that you're not. Be safe! See you at home.

Cursing, I dial her number, only to be met by her voice mail immediately. I try again, only to get the same outcome. Tapping my foot, it takes everything in me not to leave this god-forsaken bar and track her down. Actually, I'm also a little pissed off that she hasn't shared her location with me. Her bosses called and ensured she was home safe. But can a fucking phone call be enough?

Unfortunately, I know how Birdie is. She probably sat there for ten minutes trying to decide whether or not to even call me. We've known each other since we were infants, and if it hadn't been for that fateful night...

I can't let myself wonder about those horrible thoughts. She's safe. She's fine. She can wait until I get off...though, it doesn't hurt to just try one more time.

Shouting from inside the bar takes my attention away from my persistent dialing. Ending the call, I shove the damn thing away and hurry inside. I almost crash into one of the rock-for-brains bouncers, who looks caught in the headlights. We're around the same height, I'm maybe a couple inches taller at six foot two.

"What the fuck is going on?" I shout, halting everyone in their tracks. "I step outside for ten minutes and come back to a fucking shit show?"

"Man, these rowdy kids were stomping their feet on my end of the bar!" Dennis hollers as he points to a group of college girls. "Half naked, I could see her damn coochie! No offense, but I ain't wantin' to see that shit. I asked them to get on their end, which she spat in my drink!"

"Alright, wrap it up everyone," I shout, twirling a finger above my head. "We're not doing this tonight. Tabs are closing out now. Make a line at the railing and get your ID ready."

After what felt like all night, I put the rest of the glasses on the rack for tomorrow. I didn't expect tonight to turn out like this. Dennis and Paul were all too happy to make a report on the college girl who was drunk out of her mind. I took their statements, then put them in the shred box. Grown ass men acting like fucking children. I scoff at the thought alone.

Looking at the time, it's just after three in the morning.

"Fuck," I curse, running a hand through my hair. It's still damp from the dishes I washed. It catches on a few pieces, the tugs harsh enough to keep me grounded and focused.

It's fucking pathetic how my chest tightens in fear for the one woman I've been in love with since I can remember. I'm pretty sure I told our families I was going to marry her one day. She laughed at me and acted like it was nothing. In reality, the damn organ in my chest beats only for her. I've tried to call her a couple of times, but they've all gone to voice mail. Once I finally sent her a text, it didn't even push it through as delivered. So, she must have shut her phone off or let it die.

I wouldn't be surprised by either one.

Her bosses assured she'd gotten home safely. They confirmed that they dropped her off at our apartment in Gideon Lake.

Heart constricting tightly, I hastily get into my car and zoom back to the house. Traffic is light at this time, but getting stopped by a Stater is the last thing I want to do. So, I weave through the backroads until our janky complex comes into view.

Taking the stairs two at a time, my hands shake harshly, I round the corner and stop dead in my tracks. The door's slightly ajar.

Chapter Three

BIRDIE

"You're such a naughty girl," he grunts, moving my hair aside and gripping my neck tightly. Harsh bricks scrape into my cheek, the tip of my nose barely touches the rough wall. His one hand holds both of mine hostage, not letting up even while I struggle to regain control over myself.

"Get off me," I squeak through the pressure. A whimper makes its way through my tightly clenched throat. His breath is rancid against my face, almost like his mouth is rotting.

"You were wearing this short, short scrap of material. Weren't you just asking for it?"

"Birdie!" A voice shouts, body getting violently shaken. On instinct, I swing out. The person grabs my wrist, pulling me into them. Thrashing, I can't let him get me again.

"It's okay, baby bird," the masculine voice mutters. Those four words and the scent of pine are all it takes for me to crumble against him.

"I'm sorry." He continues to shush me as tears trail down my cheeks. Slowly dragging my hands between us, I ball his shirt in my fists.

"You have nothing to be sorry for. I'm sorry for not being there for you tonight." The watery giggle comes out of me before I can stop it.

"Oh, Scout," I sniffle, "you have nothing to apologize for either." He pulls away from me a bit, flicking between my eyes.

"If I'd have been here, you wouldn't have these nightmares," he counters, petting my hair gently. His fingers run through the knotted ends, untangling them gently.

"You can't save me from everything." When I first started having nightmares, I tried my best to hide them from everyone. I was too embarrassed and ashamed of myself to tell anyone what happened, let alone that my brain was forcing me to remember all of it.

Then, something just...clicked. We accidentally fell asleep on the couch watching movies one night. He'd gone up to bed, and I stayed on the sofa with a blanket draped over me. According to him, I woke up kicking and screaming my lungs out about *him*. Scout found me, scooped me into his arms, and my whimpering sleepy self admitted everything to him. I don't even remember it happening, that's how disoriented I am.

He convinced me to go back upstairs with him and to cuddle it out. When we had a hard time, we just cuddled. That's what best friends did for one another. That night, I didn't have a single nightmare. The next night, again, nothing. It was at that time we both realized that I felt more than safe with him.

This is the second time I've had to sleep without him.

"I sure as hell can try." His eyes shone with need, one that I'm not sure I'm reading right. "You have to know what you mean to me, baby bird," he whispers, leaning his forehead against mine. My eyes flutter closed on their own accord, happiness squeezing my heart.

"I don't..." I honestly don't know what to say.

"Do you not feel this?" He mutters, leaning his forehead against mine. I'm really just...stunned. "If you don't, just say *something*. Anything. Tell me it's not what I think it is."

For some fucked up reason...I can't tell him no. It's not because I *can't*.

I don't want to.

"Please," I whisper, tilting my chin ever so slightly to reach him. I know exactly what I'm asking for. Without further hesitation, he slants his plush lips over mine. The unsettled piece of my heart seems to click into place as he devours me whole. I'll admit the mountain man in front of me doesn't scare me. If anything, he seems to push my wildest dreams further than they've ever gone. Like this one. My late-night rendezvous of touching myself to his wicked smirk blossoms in front of my eyes.

Hands roam over one another, clothes gripped and yanked as we frantically try to undress each other. My shirt is the first thing to come off, catching him off guard when I'm not wearing a bra.

"Wait," he breathes and jerks himself backward, almost as if I burned him. "Wait." Running his long fingers through his thick hair, my heart hammers against my chest, threatening to jump straight into my throat.

"I-I'm sorry." I swallow thickly as I try to come to terms with the rejection. Being honest with myself, I'm not nearly in the same league as him. He's got the whole dark and broody thing going for him, while I'm just...well, me. Where he's pure muscle, I'm soft. My stomach isn't toned, my ass and thighs jiggle as I walk and show hints of cellulite. I've got small stretch scars on my butt where I grew into myself too fast. While I've tried everything I can to lose weight, it's just not coming off without medical help.

He huffs a mirthless laugh, shaking his head harshly. "Baby bird, it's not you." He plops onto the bed, dropping his head into his hands. "I didn't mean to throw myself at you. *I'm* sorry."

I can't help the ridiculous laugh that bursts out of me. I decide to throw caution to the wind. If that's not an admission of attraction, then either I'm fucking dumb or that's the sign I need. "You're an utter idiot," I giggle, throwing myself back into his arms. "I just want these nightmares to go away."

Lips land, teeth clatter, hands roam. I swear he even *growls* when his hands grasp my ass and kneed. Yanking his mouth away, he uses his nose to shove my head to the side and kiss down my neck. He sucks the skin under my ear, moving until he hits *the* spot. Grinding down on his covered cock, the friction is perfect. I could cum just like this.

"You don't know the things I'd do to you," he growls, biting my flesh harshly. One hand tangles into my hair at the base of my skull and yanks backward, jerking my head. "You'd look beautiful tied up in knots, begging to cum on my tongue, on my fingers, on my cock."

His filthy words have my hips rocking even more, his jeans barely giving me what I need now that we've shifted slightly.

"Please," I whimper, the plea continues to fall from my lips. There's a groan of satisfaction before he's flipping us over, pinning his heavy body beneath mine. I reach to tangle my hands in his hair too, when he grabs them at the wrist and yanks them above my head.

"These stay," he commands. Every instinct has me listening without fault. "What are you begging for, baby? My tongue, fingers, or cock?" Words don't seem to want to formulate in my brain. Instead, I ramble continued pleas for him to just choose something.

His hot tongue swirls my taught nipple. "I want your cock, please," I beg. He does the one thing I don't expect.

He stands, stepping several feet away. "Stay."

Chapter Four

BIRDIE

Heart jumping into my throat, I debate whether to sit up and cover myself or not. Almost like rejection, I swear my hormones jump all over the place. The only reason I'm unwavering? That simple command. My toes threaten to curl into the sheets, fingers ball into fists as I fight myself to remain unmoving.

"Do you trust me?" He questions as the button his jeans pops free. His hard erection presses harshly against his zipper, even after he releases the binding. "I need an answer. Do you trust me?"

"You know I do." A wicked smirk plasters itself on his lips. Taking several more steps away, he spins on his heel and makes a b-line to his closet.

Clattering and shuffling peaks my curiosity. Right as I make my mind up and start scooting off the bed, he comes out with several items in his arms. The possessive gleam in his eyes has me taking my place on the bed again. He doesn't say anything about the fact that I've just moved.

"I think you'd appreciate these," he assures, grabbing a small wad of rope and pulling it out. It's bright pink, unlike the usual red or black colored ones. "It's Shibari rope, so it's soft and pliant but strong. I figured you would appreciate the color choice. It was chosen just for you." Holding it out to me, he lets the smooth material caress my hand. A soft giggle escapes me at the comment. My favorite color is actually blue, but we always talk about how pink really suits my skin tone. He'd said the color made me look angelic. I remember snorting in disbelief but playing along. After some debate, we agreed that I'd only allow pink things to tie me up. I thought the conversation was simply metaphorical.

Thank goodness I was wrong.

"What other goodies do you have?" I whisper, the tone coming out more seductive than I realize. It's then I notice my thighs are tightly pressed together, trying to relieve the pressure on their own. Shuffling closer to him, he smirks at my curiosity.

"Well, I was thinking we'd start small." He undoes the rope, letting the strand unwind. "However, I think you could handle a little more than small." There's an innuendo in there somewhere but...

"And is that why I'm the only one naked?" His shirt lay discarded next to us on the floor, where all of my clothes also remain. There's a small wet spot where I was humping him like my orgasm depended on it.

Which, I suppose it did.

"I prefer to have my pants on while I pleasure you," he quips. Moving to me quickly, he doesn't give me any time to respond before I'm flipped over onto my stomach, arms stretched above my head. My poor brain spins from the rapid movement. It barely registers that he's using that silky pink rope to cuff my hands together above my head. Giving a gentle tug, he waits for my reaction. It's simple, elegant. Perfect for us.

Us. What a thought to have.

"Us," I blurt, causing him to freeze in his tying.

"What about us?" Wrapping the cord around the metal bars of the bed, he brings it back and ties a simple knot. I'll have to ask him how he learned all of this.

"You and me..." I murmur, shoving my face in the mattress. My cheeks heat rapidly at the failure of my brain to mouth filter. A tight grip is tangled in the back of my hair, pulling my head off the bed to look at him.

"What about us?" He asks again, and there's no denying the heat in his gaze.

"After this..." I can't seem to get that damn filter to spit any words out. "What happens to us?"

"Easy," he shrugs and sets my head back on the mattress gently. His fingers move hair away from my face. "You're mine after tonight, baby bird." Smashing his plush lips against mine, he dominates me from this submissive pose. Neck turned quite far, he controls every aspect of this kiss.

"Please," I whimper, the sound surprising me more than him.

"Don't worry, baby," he coos. My bottom lips gets sucked between his teeth, soft nibbles meeting the swollen flesh. "I plan to tie you to me forever." His teeth sink into the skin, and the cry of pain slips. The sharp sting is immediately soothed by his hot tongue, and a heartbeat forms in my clit.

He breezes over my hot skin with the tips of his fingers, cool air playing over me. Taking a few steps back, the male of pure muscle rounds the bed and out of my line of vision. Seconds tick by as I wait for something, anything, to happen.

"I'm going to make your cum several times before I stretch this tight pussy," he mutters, the air from his words cast over my heated core, and I jolt. A sharp swat lands on my ass. The quick shrill of pain zings up my spine before his hand smooths the spot, bringing me back to bliss.

"That's a good fucking girl." His tongue lands on my clit, and again, I can't help my hips from stuttering. The sensation is unreal. Since the *incident*, I've been too scared to have any real connections with men. Was my brain a block from reaching out? Maybe. It may also be because of the golden tanned male currently eating my pussy like it's going to be his last meal. Purely surreal. Unlike any sensation a measly vibrator can give me.

A sudden flame lights in my core.

"You like this pussy?" I mewl, rocking back into his face as much as I can. He growls onto my core, sucking my clit and pulsing it between his tongue and teeth.

"I'm going to fucking flood this cunt with my cum. You're mine, and there's no fucking changing that." A single finger sinks into me, angling and hitting *that* spot.

"Yes!" I cry and fist the rope. I attempt to pull myself on my elbows, but a quick *smack* to my ass has me face planting back into the mattress.

"Cum for me, like a good little bird." And do I fucking cum. Clouds storm my mind, masking every potential thought I could possibly have, and forcing me to ride out my pleasure. Waves upon waves crash over me as he adds another finger, working my overly sensitive clit more and more.

"Please," I sob and wiggle, trying to get him to stop. He ignores my plea for more and pulls his fingers from my pussy. Warm fingers drag from my clit to my opening...then further. Pressing a single digit to my asshole, my back bows further. Another new sensation ready to overwhelm me.

"You want me to use you like a dirty bird? Fuck and flood your cunt with my cum until I properly breed you?" Somewhere in the back of my mind, my brain is screaming that I don't have birth control. The other, less logical side is shouting in victory. "I'll stretch this tight hole and fuck it until I nearly explode, then shove my cock back into your pussy to make sure my cum takes."

I swear my brain misfires because...that idea sounds amazing right now.

Chapter Five

SCOUT

J ust as I push my thumb into her tight hole, it clamps impossibly tighter. Releasing a groan of approval, I glide my free hand over her tight globes and kneed the soft flesh between my calloused fingers. Her whimpers get rougher as my thumb pushes all the way to my last knuckle.

I pull it out, deciding our first time doesn't need to be obscene. Gripping her cheeks, I spread her fully for my viewing. Her pussy flutters, both of her tight holes clenching and releasing.

"You like that, baby bird?" I mutter, licking a single stroke from her clit to her asshole. The mumble from her is incoherent, and I can't say that I approve. Without missing a beat, I sink my teeth into her tight ass cheek.

"Shit!" She shouts and rocks forward in an attempt to get away from me. In a punishment like form, I slam two fingers inside her aching pussy and roughly find her spot.

She doesn't seem to mind. In fact, the noises she's spewing spur me on, my cock tightening even more painfully in the heavy material of my jeans as liquid gushes from her. Pouring down my fingers and onto the bed, I attempt to catch as much of it as possible, but I'm only human. Instead, I lick along her thighs and redeem some of it.

"You taste fantastic when you cum." Her entire body quakes in pleasure.

"Please, please," she chants over and over, her fists tightening and releasing the soft pink rope. Smoothing my bite away with my tongue, I soften my strokes inside her.

"I can't wait to see you in a harness of ropes," I growl, sucking her clit into my mouth for a moment. "Have your tits tied up, maybe even shinju." Reaching between her wet thighs, I roughly pinch one of her taut nipples, pulling downward.

"Yes," she gasps with a nod, desperation pouring from her words. I don't doubt that she has absolutely no idea what any of that means, but just from this moment alone...I think she'd be willing to try anything once.

With me.

"What do you want?" I tease again, knowing damn well she would bite my head off if she wasn't restrained to the bed.

"You know what I want," she snarls dangerously. My cock twitches in my jeans. I'm sure she thinks she looks like the devil, but she's more like a sweetheart.

She'll learn who the devil is before long.

"Awe, that's not how needy whores get what they want," I coo degradingly. My body freezes as hers tenses, only to have her shove her hips backwards into me harshly.

"Now," she demands.

Who am I to resist?

"What do you say?" Yanking her hips higher, I move off the bed. My jeans hit the floor heavily, and I'm right back behind her.

"Fucking *please*," she whines, nearly choking out a sob of frustration.

"I suppose since you're such a good girl..." I don't give her any time to adjust. I shove myself into her wet heat and nearly burst right then and there. She's tighter than any fucking pocket pussy I'd had. Images and visions of how she felt don't add up to the real thing.

A happy sigh escapes my innocent girl, her head resting on the pillow as I jerk out of her, only to slam balls deep. Only the whites of her eyes are visible as I use her pussy for the taking.

"You like to be fucked like my dirty slut?" I growl, my body taking over for my mind. It's as if we've been doing this for years. We just...click. The chemistry is there, active, and my balls draw into my body so tightly I might be able to taste them if they get any higher.

"Yours," she shrieks, back bowing even further as I pound her into the next week. I knew this wasn't going to fucking last long...

"This is my fucking pussy, do you understand?" I grunt, reaching between her cushioned thighs and stroking her erect nub.

"Yes!" Glee fills my chest, pride soaking through my pores.

"Tell me what you want with my cum."

"Cum in me, fuck it into me, I need your cum," she chants over and over, throwing us both over the edge simultaneously. Her screams echo around my brain as if I'm under water. Landing on her back, my teeth sink into the soft skin between her neck and shoulder, marking her as mine for everyone to see.

The desire is fucking animalistic, and I know she likes it because it launches her into another fucking orgasm.

Her pussy milks my cock of cum. I stay rooted inside of her, locked and ready to have her cervix take my sperm and turn it into something more.

Chapter Six

SCOUT

S un shining between the blinds, it casts right over my eyes. Groaning, I roll until I hit the soft, warm body of Birdie. Except, she's naked. Her beautiful body is on display for me, her hair cast over the pillow like a halo as she drools into the cover face first. The soft blanket drapes over her plush ass, her back exposed, and leaving just enough to the imagination.

Flashbacks of the last night stream through my brain like an old movie, and I can't stop the male pride from blossoming. I have no fucking clue if she's in her cycle thing or not, but it doesn't stop me from wanting to bang my chest and roar like a fucking lion.

My cock stands directly at her, waiting to sink back into her warm, wet heat. Not that I'd think she'd mind.

Last night was unlike anything I'd experienced. Not only did she let me tie her hands, she let me lay her out and tie her legs to the headboard, perfectly splaying open for me. I'd never realized how flexible she was until last night.

Though, more serious thoughts have been plaguing me this morning. One of my hands instantly reaches for her as the negativity refuses to leave me alone. My fingers trail over the smooth flesh of her back, admiring how pale and soft it is.

What if it was just one and done? Was it as good for her as it was for me? I mean, judging by the multiple orgasms I gave her, I'd sure as fuck hope it was.

Propping my head on my hand, I drag my fingers up her back to her head and tuck back a few stray hairs from her face.

"Good morning," her light brown eyes blink open, a gentle smile gracing her soft features.

"Good morning, beautiful." Smiling, I lean forward slowly, giving her plenty of time to pull away. When she doesn't, I cup her small face and plant my lips over hers. Everything about her seems perfect. She just takes everything in stride.

It's just...right.

Pulling back, she drops her head back on the pillow, giving a silent yawn. Neither one of us speaks as we soak in one another, letting the warm sun breath over us. There's still plenty of snow outside to remind us that it's still freezing, but the reprieve of the sun is one to relish on.

"I just want-" I start, just as she says "we really should-". Smiles break out even wider, a blush creeping up her neck and onto her cheeks.

"You go first," I chuckle, rolling onto my back and dragging her with me. She follows effortlessly and props her head on her hands as one of mine settles on her ass. There's this...*twinkle* in her eyes that I don't remember seeing before last night. I could be a bit biased, but it really was something special.

"Uhm, we should really talk about it," she smiles, the blush deepening even further. Nodding, I use my eyes to let her go first. "It was...unexpected to say the least."

"Baby bird, I've been dreaming about this since we met." She has the innocence to look shocked. I'm no virgin, but every girl I've been with has simply been a placeholder for her. "You've been my main priority since the beginning. Then when *it* happened..."

"Scout." I drop a single finger on her mouth, and she sucks it between her teeth. My entire body goes rigid, my deflated cock suddenly perking up and thinking it's fucking show time.

Down boy.

"Seeing you shattered, your soul almost sucked from your body...there's not a shittier feeling than knowing I wasn't able to help you. I've been making it up to you ever since. You deserve someone willing to save you from your demons, and I've been trying to prove myself worthy to you."

"You're more than worthy," she whispers, placing a kiss on my chest. I don't stop the smile making its way on my face.

"I think that's my line," I tease, tucking more strays away from her face. "I hope I've proved to you that I'm worth it. Just because I've finally got you in my arms with your heart on your sleeve doesn't mean I'm not going to keep winning you over."

"You've had my heart since we met," she reassures. She pulls herself up my body and runs her nose over mine, resting her forehead with mine.

Tightly gripping her hair, I ensure she's staring into my eyes as I lay my card on the table. "From now on, it's you and me. You're *mine*, do you hear me?" Her chin drops, mouth popping open slightly as her bottom lip gets sucked between her teeth. Using my free hand, I pull it free and bring her mouth to mine again.

There's nothing better than having the girl of your dreams in your arms. If only I knew it would last.

Chapter Seven

BIRDIE

The weeks are flying by, Scout and I are growing closer and closer. It's been five or six weeks since we've decided to move forward with each other, and it's simply unreal how quickly we've jumped into things. Future talks still scare me a little, but he reassures me that everything is going to be okay. Honestly? I believe him. He's been nothing but supportive since we've declared our like for one another. Not only that, but he's been my biggest cheerleader since we were kids! I can't imagine a life without him here, and it makes everything more real. My perspective is shifting.

"I'm back, and I've brought food!" The front door closes as Scout makes himself known. Laughing, I slide off the stool, catching him in all his glory. His shirt is plastered to his body, emphasizing how well taken care of his body is.

"Did you go to the gym?" I question, my tongue darting from my mouth to wet my lips. This man is delectable.

"Why? Can you tell?" Setting the take-out food on the coffee table, he flexes his arms in one of those muscle daddy poses.

"I mean, the fact that your shirt is practically a second skin..." I trail, too damn distracted as he practically prowls to me.

"You like?" Leaning down to my neck, he inhales deeply. The exhale skates teasingly over my skin, a shiver coasting down my spine in desire.

"I love." He pulls back, our eyes not moving from one another. It's the first time I've hinted at anything remotely close to the L word.

"Good." Scooping me into his arms, I gleefully laugh and wrap my legs around his waist. His lips slant over mine, our kiss mixed with lust and smiles.

"I've missed you," he mutters against my lips. My smile grows impossibly wider, and he might as well be kissing teeth. Instead of responding, I tighten my grip even more on his hulking form and push myself further into the kiss. I attempt to say everything on my mind through it, hoping he'll silently understand that I'm falling more and more in love with him every day.

Loosening my legs just a little, I lower until I'm rubbing myself over his cock. He doesn't flinch, rocking into me more as we barely make it to the couch.

"You sure you don't want to eat first?" He rumbles, and I float through the air as he drops me unceremoniously onto the cushions.

"Who wants to fuck with a full stomach?" I scoff sassily, grabbing a fist full of his hair and yanking him down to me. He doesn't deny me what I want and settles between my open thighs, grinding into my covered pussy with his covered cock. The musky, woodsy scent wafts off him, like he just put deodorant on after working out. That, or he just naturally smells like a fucking God. Either one works for me, to be honest.

Slowly, he works my clothing off of me. I knew I should have waited for him naked. Rolling my eyes at the thought, he grabs my shirt in the middle and pulls. The flimsy material splits into two effortlessly. My breasts bounce in their confines, waiting to be devoured. Thankfully, they don't have to wait too long. Lifting me up slightly, he reaches behind my back and unclasps it.

"You couldn't have taken my shirt off like a normal person?" I tease, shimmying myself out of the bra.

"I could have, but would it have made your cunt clench?" Welp, I can't argue with that logic.

Burying his face between my small tits, he licks the salty skin until he sucks one of the taut buds into his warm mouth. I'm not even sure what noises I'm making at this point, but I know it's spurring him on. His warm tongue slides over the peak before his teeth clamp down on it. Hissing, my fingers grip his hair tighter and attempt to yank him away. A wicked gleam catches my gaze, and he lets me pull him back, not without taking my nipple with him between his teeth.

"Shit!" There's a fine line where pain meets pleasure, and I didn't realize this was what it felt like. The bouncy flesh giggles as it returns to its normal spot. Lashing out, his tongue smooths over the painful spot.

"Did my greedy girl like that?" He growls against my stomach, waiting for the green light.

"Yes," I whimper, wiggling my hips to give him a hint of what I'm wanting.

"I have a better idea." Pushing himself off the couch, he takes a solid step backward. I can't stop the groan of annoyance from leaving my throat. "I think you're really going to like it," he taunts, wiggling his fingers as he waits for me to grab his hand. Glaring at his handsome face may as well be a sin. Instead, I huff and grasp his calloused hand in my softer one.

"This better be good." He just chuckles, dragging me in the opposite direction of the bedroom. "Where are you going?"

"You'll see." The look on his face is enough to stop my next impeding questions in their tracks. I follow along silently, and we stop outside a bedroom door. Opening it, I can't stop my jaw from dropping.

"Holy..." Letting go of my hand, he presses it to my lower back and pushes me forward. There's a bunch of different stuff that I didn't even know existed. One of them looks like a fucking saw horse with padding on it. It shines, so obviously it's clean, and it looks like it's leather.

"What do you think?" I look at him over my shoulder, trying to gauge his own reaction. His lip is tucked between his teeth, hands stuffed in the pockets of his gym shorts. There's a look on his face that I can't quite place. Maybe longing? Suspense? Hope?

"I mean," I span my arms out, "this is like my dream jungle." A shit eating grin opens over his face. "This is what you turned the third bedroom into?"

"You said I have freedom over it," he shrugs, grabbing my hand and bringing me closer to his body.

"I didn't expect you to make a freaking dungeon," I giggle, unable to help myself from reaching out and touching the silky pink sheets. "It's all pink, black, and blue," I say, though it comes out more like a question.

"I'm respecting your favorite color, my favorite color on you, and black is what most of the toys come in." The body cross in the corner is painted black with pink leather cuffs strapped to the corners. The four poster bed is black and pink, but there's this honeycomb style grid at the end of the bed that's dark blue. It sounds like an odd color match, but it really works.

"I love it." I turn to kiss him, but he takes a single step back.

"You have five minutes to explore and one minute to choose the things you'd like for me to use on you." His watch makes a beep, and I take off. There's so much to see, it's unreal.

Running around the room, I grab everything I think I'd like, with a smile on my face. A louder *beep beep* rings around the room. Dumping all my findings on the bed, he takes a step over and inspects them.

"Good girl," he growls, striding back to me. With quick work, my hair is skilfully braided and pulled away from my face. "I want you naked and on your knees by the door by the time I get back."

Chapter Eight

BIRDIE

I don't get to answer as he strides out of the room, letting the door latch closed. I only have my skirt and panties on, which I make quick work of discarding on a spare chair behind the door. Kneeling by the door, I try to figure out what to do with my body. After a moment, I decide on setting them on my thighs, the backs of my hands facing upward.

The audible door click pulls me from my thoughts, and I keep my eyes down. I've seen enough porn movies to know we don't make eye contact.

"You were very close," he coos, taking my wrist and turning it over. I do the other side on my own, keeping my eyes down. "Such a good girl, baby bird."

His hand pets my head, and while I want to scream at him to get his hand off my head, he smooths it down my back. Twisting my braid in his fist, he gently but sufficiently tugs me from my knees. Leading me over to the giant X, he hikes me up onto the foot rests.

"Be a good girl, and don't move, hmm?" Raising a brow, I can see the war behind his eyes. It's a mix between lust, love, and something else.

Power?

"Okay," I breathe out with a nod. Before I can blink, a sharp swat lands on my outer thigh, right by my butt. "Oh!" The sting is immediately soothed by his large hand.

"You will address me as 'Sir' or 'Master'. Do I make myself clear?" His eyes hold a predatory glare, one that has me fucking melting at the post.

"Yes," I pause, trailing my eyes down his chiseled body, "master." Like a snake, he moves effortlessly and gracefully, yet he strikes quickly as he fastens me into the contraption.

He steps back to admire me for a moment, then turns on his heels to go to the bed where I dropped all the things. Waiting with bated breath, his fingers skim over the materials one by one, casually throwing glances over his shoulder. I know he's trying to get a rise out of me, and it's working.

Just as I'm about to scream at him to hurry the hell up, he grabs a hot pink and black whip thing that has many little...strings? Tentacles?

"Do you know what this is?" He questions, rolling the leather in his hand.

"No." I shake my head, remaining silent while he waits. "Master," I quickly add after I realize my mistake. "No, master." He doesn't seem to mind my little slip up, because he moves on.

"This is a flogger." A wicked gleam hits his eyes as a matching smirk makes its way onto his mouth. "These are tresses," he rolls the tentacle things, "this is the neck," he grabs where the tresses meet the stick piece, "and this is the shaft."

Who knew floggers had anatomy?

"Thank you, Master." There's a sense of...freedom I get while standing here. He continues to talk about how it's used, and things of that nature, but all I can think about is what it'll feel like when it makes contact. Will it welt? Will he like it? The books make it sound a lot easier than it probably is. I mean my pain tolerance is higher than most people-

"Attention!" He commands, and I'm immediately pulled out of my thoughts. "You ignoring me, baby bird?"

"No, Master!" I declare, shaking my head.

"Good, because I would hate to punish you for failing a pop quiz." A lump grows in my throat, thick and heavy, sitting in the way of air flow.

Thankfully, he doesn't give me that quiz, instead dragging the material over my flush skin. It's cool to the touch and goose bumps explode in its wake.

He teases between my thighs with the tresses, switching from one side to the other as I try to wiggle my hips and get him right where I want him.

Without warning, he whips the flogger down on the inside of my thigh. A burning sting jerks my body before he repeats it on the other thigh.

"You get as much as I say you get," he admonishes, another sharp smack landing. "Do you understand?"

"Yes, Master," I gasp, my body buzzing with an unnatural amount of adrenaline. He doesn't give the usual praise, instead taking it and swatting my outer thighs. It's sharp, brinking on the edge of too much.

Just as I'm about to tell him as much, he backs up. There's an underlying possession in his eyes, one that makes me want to jump off this damn cross and devour him. It's almost unnerving.

"Look at you, marked so prettily for me," he growls, setting the flogger back on the bed before grabbing the plug-in wand I picked. "I believe you deserve a reward for taking it so nicely." Rolling it around in his hand, it almost looks like he's trying to debate something.

I know better than to say anything without being spoken to, so I keep my lips zipped. Although I'm completely new to this, I can't help but feel as though I'm exactly where I need to be.

"You get to pick, baby bird. Wand with the dildo machine or do you want the wand with my cock?"

"Cock, please," I beg. My brain is so damn foggy and filled with only thoughts of him, things that he should absolutely stop hesitating on doing. "Please, Master. I need it." Instead of giving me what I want, he stands there and waits. I disintegrate into a standing and cuffed puddle of pleas.

"That's a good girl, yes you do," he agrees, smirking devilishly. "Now, what should I fill first? Your pussy, or your ass?"

Instead of using his cock like he said, he shoves his fingers straight into my pussy. He pulls me to the point of detonating before pushing me away from it. Again and again, I get close then get shut down.

I don't even know if I'm using words at this point. It's more likely that I'm just wiggling with noises that range from high pitched screams to low rolling groans. My orgasm races up my spine, just about to peak-

"What the fuck!" I shriek and jerk against the restraints in anger. He only *tsks* while shutting off the wand. The three fingers that were stuffed inside me are suddenly shoved in his mouth with a satisfied groan.

"Now, now, baby bird. You'll eventually get what you want, but I'll give you what you need." Dropping the wand, he releases my hands from the links above my head and slowly lowers them to my sides. He admires the red welts on my body, obviously getting more aroused.

Dropping to his knees in front of me, his nose gets stuffed between my thighs and inhales deeply. My hands grip his hair harshly, tugging him closer, and when he laps at the juices covering my core. He pushes me to the brink once again before pulling away. I don't even get a chance to scream my frustrations. He's up on his feet and tossing me over his shoulder, then I'm floating for a mere moment before I hit softness.

Heaviness drops over me before I'm being filled in one swift shove. I can't breathe, the pleasure overwhelming enough to force my orgasm from my body.

"Too much," I gasp, clawing at his back for some type of leverage. Liquid meets my nails, but I don't think either one of us cares. His hips slam against mine as he chases his own pleasure, hand gripping my throat and holding me in place. It stops me from getting shoved up the bed, too.

"You want this perfect pussy stuffed full of my cum, don't you?" He grunts, and there's slight tilt in his hips before the tip of his cock rubs against the *perfect* spot.

"Oh god," I cry, reaching between us to rub my clit.

"God isn't here baby, but I'll gladly rule your world." His lips plant over mine, and I shatter on a silent scream, his hand tightening further on the sides of my neck. I swear he's saying something, but I can't hear it past being shattered beneath him. White flashes behind my closed eyes, my head floats as if there's not even a bed beneath us.

There's nothing more than us, and I wouldn't have it any other way.

Chapter Nine

FOUR WEEKS LATER

BIRDIE

"Fucking hell," I grumble, resting my head on the cool bar. Viviana rounds the corner on her tablet.

"Woah," she gasps and comes up next to me. "You're looking green." She places a gentle hand on my forehead, and I can't stop the bubbling laugh of frustration from coming out.

"I feel green. There's this platter of cheeses that isn't sitting well with my nostrils. I've never had an issue before," I sigh, rubbing my hands over my eyes.

"Do you need to go home?" Her eyes shine with concern. Shaking my head, I sit up and my knees threaten to collapse.

"No, I think I need some fresh air." On shaky legs, I grab my coat and stand in front of the door. Snow lay peacefully on the ground, opposite of my stomach which is currently mimicking a storm.

"Let me know if you need to go home, we can find coverage." Nodding, I step into the cool February air. Immediately, I feel better. There's nothing more satisfying than being able to cool off after being warm.

"Hey, Viv said you weren't feeling good?" Sofia says, and I jump slightly, not even realizing she came up to me.

"I'm alright, just a little under the weather." Smiling, I know she can see right through it. It's plastic and doesn't reach my eyes. It wouldn't take a rocket scientist to realize it wasn't real.

"Mmmm," she nods and stands silently next to me for a few minutes. "How's everything going with Scout?"

"Oh, they're great," I sigh, blushing deeply at the thought of him. When he said he'd deem himself worthy, he's gone above and beyond with everything he's done. I made it clear a few times that he's done more than enough, but for him, it won't be enough.

"You being safe?" Turning toward me, she reaches out a hand with a small blue package sticking out. I'm sure I look freaking shocked because she just smiles.

"I'm not..." I can't even finish the sentence because I know it might be true. We've not been careful, at all, and he's made it abundantly clear his intentions for my womb.

"Just take it. If it's negative, I'm sending you home for a couple days."

"And if it's positive?" I swallow thickly, emotions already gripping my throat tenfold.

"If it's positive, we'll sit down and find you a good obstetrician." Without saying another word, I grab the small plastic stick and make my way to the bathroom.

Scout talked about doing this together, me peeing on the stick and letting him be there with me. Something about how it will make it all better. Knowing that I need to know if I'm basically contagious or not, I don't have the luxury.

Well, I could just go home for the day and be done, but something in my gut is telling me to stay put.

Instead, I settle on giving him a call. It goes straight to voicemail. I try again, where it rings a few times and goes to voicemail again. Sending him a text, I wait about five minutes. He read it, but hasn't responded. Opening his location, it shows he's at the dive bar. It's too early, and he didn't mention anything about working early today.

Shrugging it off, I do my business and stick the cap back on the stick. I set a quick timer on my phone, and pace the bathroom. It's a stand alone, so I have room.

What if it's positive? Negative? How will Scout react? I know he'll be upset that I did it without him, but I'd rather not have to wait. There's so much potential that everything could go to shit...no, I can't think like that. It's weird to think I didn't see the signs before. I mean, every woman's boobs hurt after menstruation, right? Or is it just me? I guess they don't usually hurt this long. Also,

I haven't been sick since I was in highschool, and I don't think I've puked since before that.

A loud knock startles me, and I realize my timer is going off for the past minute. "It's just me. Let me know if you need anything."

I shakily respond. Just as I'm about to look at the stick, my phone vibrates with a text from an unknown number. Furrowing my brows, I open it to see a photo loading through. Just as I go to close it as spam, it pops through.

It stops me cold in my tracks.

Chapter Ten

SCOUT

"Look, I'm not interested, okay?" I say, pulling away from the pushy female. Her jean shorts are practically painted on her, but the only woman I can think of is Birdie. *My baby bird.*

"Come on, Scotty, I'm only looking for a good time, not a long one. The other girls said you were a good fuck, and I'm here for it."

"My name is Scout, not 'Scotty', and no means no. If the roles were reversed, you'd go crying to the cops that I tried to rape you or some shit. I've got a girl waiting for me at home, so take a hint, chick. *No.*" That doesn't seem to do the trick either. Instead, it makes her more fiery.

"Come on, you know you want to," she drops her boobs on the counter of my bar, and I can't suppress the growl. Unfortunately, she takes it as a sexual one, not a predatory one.

Before I can blink, she has a hand in my hair and is pulling me in for a kiss. She tastes like cheap vodka. Grabbing her face, I gently pry her away from me. Even if I was just sexually assaulted, I'm not going to go in handcuffs for slapping this chick. That's the way the world works, and I plan to make Birdie take a stick test tonight.

"Got it!" One of the friends from her posse shouts, cheering loudly for her friend.

"Get the fuck out of my bar! All of you," the fiery owner calls, grabbing a cloth and whipping it at the girl. "You don't get to assault my workers for a quick pic. I don't care if his dick is the size of an elephant trunk, you need to leave. You're banned from coming back."

"But your bar is the only good one in town!" She shrieks, hands on her hips defiantly as her foot stomps petulantly.

"Should have thought about that before attacking one of my bartenders. You and your little posse have three seconds to leave before I call the cops on you and report the assault."

"Fuck, fine!" The group of girls take off at lightning speed, obviously not wanting to get charged with something stupid. I doubt it would even hold up in court, but that's besides the point.

Knuckles rap on the bartop, and I catch sight of Massimo. He's made himself more known around the bar, and he's been trying to recruit me into his...stuff. I have no desire to get twisted in that, but he provides an outlet that I've not been given before.

A deep rooted anger boils under my skin, one that almost had me lashing out at people I love. With him, I've been able to take my aggression out on men deserving of it. Traitors, spies, the like.

Jerking his head, I stalk down to his side of the bar. "Boss gave the green light for you to take off." I don't need to hear anything else. I close myself out and follow him outside.

"What do we have tonight?" I slide into his shiny car, admiring the leather like always.

"Some idiots who think they can get one over on me." We both roll our eyes, and he takes off. My mind remains blank as I do my best to not overthink everything. I'll have to tell Birdie about the chick who threw herself on me, I don't want one of these idiots to tell her without me. That's how the rumor-mill and shit starts.

Pulling into the warehouse, we both saunter over to the guards who don't even look at us. Instead, they stare out into the abyss and wait for someone to try and invade the territory. I don't understand it, but the less I know, the better.

"Don't kill them," Massimo warns as we make our way to the dungeon area. I only grunt in response. I haven't killed anyone yet, yet I've gotten pretty damn close on a couple occasions. I'd have to join whatever group he runs if I did.

No thanks.

"Well, well, look who it is." Whirling around, *he* sits there, acting smug and as if the world can't touch him even though he's tied to the chair with a chain looped around his neck.

"What the fuck is he doing here?" My fists clench tightly, nails creating crescents until I'm sure my calloused flesh is bleeding. Massimo smirks, a single shoulder lifting and dropping.

"A certain female who seems to be very special to my wife and her boss disclosed some...interesting information. Viv and I agreed that it would be best if you have first dibs."

Jaw dropping from the tight hinge, I simply stare at the man before me. There has to be some type of double standard, something he wants in return. So, I voice it.

"Nope, no strings attached. This is for the girl," he assures, his head tilting over to the man who stole the light from my girl for a few years. He's the reason she wasn't able to breathe without flinching for so long.

"I'm here because of a whore?" He booms, laughing like it's the most hysterical thing in the world. What the stupid guy doesn't understand is that I won't kill him, but I'll take him right to the brink. "Which whore was it, huh? Oh, I bet it was the pretty brunette? Or was she blond? Or-" My fist slams into his ugly face, the obvious crack of his bone rattles in my ears. A deep inhale has my blood calming slightly, the soreness of my knuckles slowly soothing the beast trying to crawl out of me.

"It's too bad you don't remember who it is," Massimo *tsks*, a few things clattering onto the metal table. It's the work supplies I've collected over the months of working with him. He sweeps a hand over it all before taking a step back.

Grabbing his hair, I wrench his head backward, letting him stare up into my devilish face. While I can't look in a fucking mirror to see what he sees, I can guarantee that he's staring at the face of the devil.

"You know, I thought you died," I begin, shoving his head forward. The chair jolts beneath him as it threatens to either break or topple. "You didn't show your face around here for so long, yet here you are. Sitting in the cave of your worst nightmare."

"I've not had a single nightmare about you," he lamely spits out. Hand tightly wrapping around his throat from behind, the choking sound immediately indicates he's struggling to breathe.

"I would say that hurts my feelings, but..." I trail off, holding out a hand. A zippo is placed on my palm. Flipping it open, the flame blazes to life. Bringing it in front of his face, the guys around us chuckle as they stare at his tortured expression.

I release his throat and come around in front of him without the fire dying. Bringing it to his eyes, he tries to wiggle and break the rope holding him, the chain clattering on the chair as he fights it.

"This is going to hurt a lot more." His head tips back to try and avoid it, but he's as far extended as he can go. Burning the lashes on his eye, the heat isn't enough to melt his skin, but enough to singe the hairs to the root and burn the lid. He hisses but doesn't scream. I don't need him to scream just yet. I need him to hurt, slow and tortured.

His other eye holds the same fate, his eyes squeezed as tightly as they'll get. Eyebrows next, then a blow torch is replacing the simple lighter.

"Do you remember a girl named Birdie? The one you stole virginity from?" I growl, firing the torch. He doesn't respond, the only reaction he gives is a subtle lift of his non-existent eyebrows. "So, you do!" I clap in mock joy, earning a glare from the man.

"Fuck you!" He spits again, trying and failing to escape the confines.

"I don't know if you know this, but you won't be leaving here alive," Massimo taunts. Glancing over at him, his body leans casually against the far wall.

"You'll pay for this!" Another round of laughs taunts the guy, while I get to work.

Firstly, I relish in his screams as his hair goes up in flames. The sensitive flesh that is usually covered by the dead skin blazes hotly, the smell of burning flesh makes my beast simultaneously relax and roar. No blood drips since the veins are basically being cauterized.

Eyes dropping, he starts passing out. One of Massimo's men injects him with something as his eyes pop open almost immediately.

This fucker is in for a long night.

Chapter Eleven

BIRDIE

Positive. It's fucking positive. Not only that, but now my world is turning upside down.

"It's probably not what it seems," Viv implores, staring at the photo with me. I haven't moved, barely even breathing. I don't know what to think, what to say.

One life changing event after the other. I thought it was going to be the turning point for us, the one thing he's talked about and literally worked at. Now, the truth seems to crash into me like an avalanche.

"It's pretty fucking clear," I sob, my throat aching from puking and sputtering in disbelief.

"Look, Birdie, his hand is on her shoulder, fingers open. He's trying not to touch her!" Sofia comments, zooming in on it.

Words don't register, the photo seems to have scarred behind my eyes when I close them. I pull the phone from them, trying for the twentieth time to call him.

"Hey, you've reached Scout. Please leave-" I push the end button, frustration breaking the walls of my sadness. What if I was on the fucking side of the road dying? What happened to being there for me?

"I'm going to take a walk." I don't give them a chance to tell me otherwise, I just take off. My muscles are sore from the crying and throwing up, yet the frigid air and movement eases some of it. Keys jingle in my pocket as I round the corner to the car lot, and my frazzled brain decides that a car ride is exactly what I need to clear my head.

Scout decided it would be good for me to take it, saying he had other things going. Apparently, it was going and screwing another female.

Opening the car, I slide in and white-knuckle grip the steering wheel. Anger and resentment build up my throat, and I release a scream that says it all. I scream for the fetus inside me, I scream for the girl who thought life was happier for her. I scream for everything that has done me wrong in my life.

Without another thought, I press down on the gas and floor it from the gravel. Looking in the rearview, the girls run after me, one holding a phone to her ear and talking rapidly.

I push the accelerator harder, willing the car to go faster. It does exactly as I want it to, swerving around corners and drifting on the dirt.

It's idiotic, reckless, but my heart feels empty.

Dead.

A single hand drops to my stomach, almost on instinct as I slow down. I have another being to think about, care for. Even if the person involved in it decided that we aren't enough.

I'm not enough.

Pulling over on the side of the two lane dirt road, I contemplate my next move. I don't even know where to go from here. I search for my phone and pat myself down, only to realize I don't have it on me. It must have dropped it during my walk or something.

"What the fuck are you doing, Birdie?" I mutter, leaning my head against the steering wheel. I'm better than this. Men don't dictate how I live my life. If he wants to go be with someone, baby bean and I will make it work. I know it.

My stomach is flat, which it will be for a while, but I think about the few months from now when I'll start getting a little round belly that's growing him or her. I wonder if they'll have light brown eyes like me or if they'll have light brown hair. I imagine what their first words might be, how many months they'll be when they walk.

I don't know, but I can say that I'm more than happy to know that this little bird and I will be just fine.

Taking several deep breaths, I decide to go back to the vineyard. I'm not really sure where I am, but I can cruise for a while and hope for the best. It will hopefully give me more time to collect myself.

Checking the mirrors, the coast is clear as I go to turn the car around. Putting it in reverse, I scoot back as far as possible before checking again and pulling into the road.

What I don't see is the flash of black flying toward me until the last second, coming out of thin air. Screaming in terror, I fumble to get the car in reverse, but I don't have time to react. The other vehicle slams into my door at high speeds, the crunch of metal on metal shrieking into my ears. The airbags don't deploy, and the seatbelt tears into my throat and waist.

White noise fills my head as my neck whips to the side, pain shooting through my head. Time stops, and I suspend in air for a moment and jerk when the car slams onto the ground before floating again. My body feels weightless, painless as I suspend. The car drops to the ground again, and my nose slams into the steering wheel. A moment of pain raptures through my skull, and it's as if my life ceases to exist.

The End.

Crisis Hotlines

I f you or someone you love are in need of emergency assistance, do not hesitate to call your local emergency number. Professionals are there to assist you as needed. All hotlines are FREE.

National Sexual Assault Hotline/Support Lines:

Australia: 1800 737 723

Canada: 604-255-6344

Germany: 08000116016

USA: 1-800-656-4673 or 877-995–5247

UK: 0808 500 2222

Suicide and Crisis Hotlines:

Australia: 13 11 14

Canada: 519-416-486-2242

Germany: 0800-181-0721

UK: 08457-90-90-90

USA: (800) 723-8255 or Dial 988

Crisis Textline:

Canada: Text HOME to 686868 for Self-Harm Help

USA: Text CONNECT to 741741 for Self-Harm Help

UK: Text SHOUT to 85258 for Self-Harm Help

About the Author

Lexi Gray is an Alaskan-Based author with several years of freelance editing under her belt. Ms. Gray has also dabbled in narrating, which can be found on Audible. She's had a passion for writing at an early age; however, started out in helping authors develop their writing skills and bringing languid movement and passion to their works. Her unique voice shines through her works, using emotion-based writing and hitting subjects that may present as taboo. Ms. Gray utilizes critical thinking and good, dirty and dark humor to get through it all.

Her hope is that when readers pick up her works, or the works of others she's helped along the way, they'll be stuck with their nose in it.

Ms. Gray herself enjoys reading dark romance, but also loves to dive into a dirty RomCom or two. From her own past experiences, she hopes to use her books as a sense of learning for those who read it, even if they end up only holding it with one hand along the way...IYKYK.

You can check out updates along the way on her Instagram:

@AuthorLexiGray or on her website at AuthorLexiGray.com

Also By

Satan on Wheels by Lexi Gray is a slow-burn, enemies to loves, motorcycle club thriller that you don't want to miss! Action packed full of fan-favorite tropes and triggers!

Don't forget, smut starts on page one! It's book one of the Rubber Down Duology.

Satan's Naughty List is book two of the Rubber Down Duology. Another action packed motorcycle club story, featuring your favorite duo from book one! This is an RH, MM/MMF love story. HEA guaranteed.

Again, smut starts in chapter one!

Printed in the USA
CPSIA information can be obtained
at www.ICGtesting.com
CBHW040741100124
3298CB00022B/107

9 798988 830368